13 MINUTES

13 MINUTES

JEFF LYONS

Storygeeks
Press

13 Minutes

ISBN: 978-0-9970663-3-3 (pbk)

ISBN: 978-0-9970663-4-0 (mobi)

ISBN: 978-0-9970663-5-7 (epub)

Cover art by Tracy Lyn

Interior design by Jeff Lyons

Give feedback on the book at:

info@storygeekspress.com

First Edition

Printed in the U.S.A

DEDICATION

This is for loyal readers past, present, and future.
Because without you, what's the point?

ACKNOWLEDGMENTS

The author would like to thank the following individuals for their support, help, encouragement, patience, infinite patience, faith, trust, belief, handouts, generosity, and small petty crimes undertaken to promote the success of this book.

• *Charlene DeLong* and *David Allan*—thank you for being trusted beta readers, editors, and telling me the truth.

FICTION

Jack Be Dead: Revelation (bk #1)

13 Minutes

Terminus Station

The Abbess (coming)

NONFICTION

Anatomy of a Premise Line: How to Use Story and Premise Development for Writing Success

Rapid Story Development: How to Use the Enneagram-Story Connection to Become a Master Storyteller (coming)

Rapid Story Development: The Storyteller's Toolbox Volume One

RAPID STORY DEVELOPMENT E-BOOK SERIES

#1: Commercial Pace in Fiction and Creative Nonfiction

#2: Bust the Top Ten Creative Writing Myths to Become a Better Writer

#3: Ten Questions Every Writer Needs to Ask Before They Hire a Consultant

#4: Teams and Ensembles: How to Write Stories with Large Casts

CONTENTS

13 MINUTES

Even without eyes she had a clear sense of the place. She could "hear the color," "see the sound," "feel the imbalance," lyrical metaphors for trusting not people but the environment. She could never get those little phrases out of her head, probably because they had been beaten into her so well. Her old drill instructor spoke in poetry and punched in prose. "The lie of sight," he loved to remind her. "Trust your nose, trust your gut—your eyes will get you killed."

The black sack over her head was designed to keep out the light, to obscure the one sense most easily fooled. That was fine. She rarely believed her eyes anyway: a lesson well learned. Her most primal sense, the one wired straight into the lizard part of her brain, smelled the fear. The smell told her she was screwed. It also told her she was not alone.

As to the why, that question had barely made its way into her consciousness. How she had been nabbed, bagged, and dumped into this place was something she could scarcely get her head around.

She knew that there were only a few people she knew capable of taking her by surprise, let alone subduing her—and they were dead.

But the *who* and the *why* would have to wait; her training and her gut told her that now was about just staying alive.

As she lay on a hard floor, her honed senses of smell and hearing told her there was more than one person in the room: both men and women. The women were easy to detect. There were two different perfumes in the air, just enough fragrance for her nose to pick them out of the mixed scents of sweat, fear, and urine. Clearly not military. Civilian? *What the hell were civilians doing here?*

The men were also easy to sense. The movement she heard around her felt nervous, skittish, the kind of motions dogs make when they are caged and pace back and forth. Women tend to stand still, consider things, be less twitchy. Also, the sour breath and general man-stink was recognizable anywhere: in training barracks, in the field, or in the dark with a hood over your head.

There was also the smell of iron and the tang of blood in the air: fresh blood. Her blood she knew, as she pulled on the cords cutting into the flesh of her ankles and wrists. Of course, it was her blood. Good lubricant: she could eventually use it to work her hands free. She might have to break a bone or two in one of her hands in order to slip through the ties, but she'd done it before; she could do it again. If she lived long enough to try.

They were close, too close. She could hear their breathing, rapid, high in their chests, bodies geared for emotional flight but with nowhere to go. One breathing pattern was different. A woman maybe, but no—this one smelled like a male, his breathing deeper, steady breaths. Perhaps more training than the others, and he was focused on her. He was behind her, to the right. She would have to take him first. Suddenly someone grabbed the bag and a clump of her hair and pulled quickly, removing both.

Her head jerked back with the pull and the pain. She remained face down. A bright, searing light blinded her. Not the clean light of day but the dirty, green light of bad fluorescence. Just as she thought: indoors, enclosed, imprisoned. Someone knelt in front of her. One of the women. She squinted and raised her eyes to see.

Now she got a look at part of the room. White floor, white walls, empty. There was a video monitor embedded in a far wall and next to it an old-fashioned digital clock that looked more like an old-fashioned, oversized alarm clock. But the face showed "oo:oo:oo" in deep red numbers. Why a clock—not a clock, a timer? And the woman, blond, hair pulled back into a messy ponytail, wearing jeans and a frumpy blouse.

"Hey. I'm Ruby. I'm not going to hurt you. I can undo your hands and feet. Would you like to sit up? Might be more comfortable." Ruby leaned forward, grabbed her by the shoulders and gently lifted her off the floor to a sitting position. Ruby leaned down close enough that she could have used her mouth to rip out Ruby's throat. But then what? She was still tied up like a calf at a Texas rodeo. She did not resist. The time would come. Right now, she at least had a better tactical view. Her survival percentage had just increased substantially.

"Ruby—back off! Don't be stupid!" The man with the slower breathing was hostile, had a British accent and a commanding voice. The others, one woman and two men backed up a couple of paces.

"Don't be silly, Tully. She's fine. She's just scared like the rest of us. Like you were when you were thrown in here bound with a bag on your head." Ruby's voice was surprisingly centered for someone scared. She was resisting Tully's authority, not in-your-face rebellion but resisting.

Whoever they were, they were not a trained team or coordinated in any way. All prisoners? Yes, they were all captives. This changed things considerably.

Ruby finished untying her hands and feet, and helped her to sit up, and then gently backed off to a safe distance. She ignored Tully but still had some caution in her. She was beginning to like this Ruby. There was strength in her.

"What I was, Ruby dear, was bloody pissed off. I was not scared. Let us all be clear on that, thank you very much." Tully harrumphed and sat in one of the plastic chairs to pout, crossing his arms across his chest defiantly.

Finally she had a clear view of the room and all of its occupants. The room was rectangular, maybe thirty feet wide and twenty feet long. Everything was white: floors, walls, ceiling. The worn, white tiles of the floor extended halfway up each of the walls. The monitor and timer hung on one wall but nothing else. The room was sealed, except for a single door at the far end. A door with no knob. Five white plastic chairs were strewn around the room, the cheap kind you can buy at neighborhood garden shops or home improvement box stores. And there were cameras, embedded in the ceiling so you couldn't knock them out or disable them, say with a hard blow from a cheap plastic chair. She had no doubt that room's resemblance to a butcher's shop was not accidental.

Ruby leaned down and offered her hand. "Hi. I'm Ruby," she giggled. "Sorry, I'm repeating myself. I just told you my name. I'm from California." The others watched, unsure, cautious, waiting. Ruby stood her ground, keeping eye contact: she was going to get that handshake, that was clear. If she refused the handshake, then the group would never trust her. It would be seen as a symbolic "up yours," and she would get no cooperation from any of them if she needed it. Not shaking set up a potentially adversarial relationship, but it also showed she was independent, a leader. This might prove valuable later on. If there was a later on. Shaking, on the other hand, showed a sense of unity, inclusion, *I'm one of you.* Unity might be the only thing that would keep both her and them alive. She looked at Ruby and the others with calculating eyes. They were all scared, except Tully. He was bored. He was going to be a problem. The choice was clear.

She reached up and took Ruby's hand. "Mae."

Ruby used the handshake to help Mae stand up, "See, I don't bite." From the sidelines Tully chimed in, "It's not you she should be worried about, is it?"

A middle-aged African American man stepped up. "Michael, Cleveland, Ohio."

Then, a fifty-something Indian. "Sanjay, Mumbai, India."

A thirtyish hipster with a thick Mandarin accent got right up into Mae's face. Her grip was strong and her gaze defiant, "Ling, New York City. Why do people introduce themselves and then say where they're from? Who the fuck cares?"

Mae gave back what she got, "I don't." She let go and smirked as she walked away.

Everyone looked at Tully, waiting for him to get up and play nice: no such luck. While lying trussed up on the floor, Mae had been the outlier. Now, everyone was on Mae's side of the room, and Tully was alone in his chair, every bit outside looking in. It was clear from the look on his face that he recognized a new dynamic was forming. He got up and moved tentatively toward the others. Mae smiled to herself. *Nobody likes being on the outside—except me.*

Mae spoke directly to him. "What did you mean?"

"Mean? About what?" Tully replied. There may have been a question mark at the end of his reply, but it wasn't a question.

"When you suggested Ruby wasn't the one with the teeth I should be afraid of."

Tully laughed. "Did you get a look at that goon that brought you here?"

"No. I had a bag over my head!"

"We all had bags over our heads," Ling interjected.

Tully ignored Ling and focused on Mae. "Where were you when they took you?"

This Mae remembered well. When it happened it had been fast, quiet, painful, and faceless. Whoever did this to her knew her skill set and exactly how to take her out. Something like this had only happened to her once before in her life, during the war, and she promised herself *never again*. So much for promises.

Granted, she had to admit that this time there was no reason to have her guard up, but that's always when the unexpected happened in her line of work—when you're sleeping, having sex, taking a shower, or in her case putting groceries into the trunk of a car. An old

Ford Econoline van pulled up behind her, its door slid open, and two freakishly tall men dressed in black coveralls and combat boots jumped out and came toward her in a rush. She remembered their movements as beautifully synchronized, ballet-like; their timing impeccable, and their execution flawless.

Even in the midst of being mugged, she appreciated well-trained machines. She should know; she used to be just like them. Trapped between her car and theirs (obviously part of the plan), there was nothing to do but kick testicles and gouge eyes out. But her kicking met nothing fleshy. Instead, the top of her shoe slammed into tight muscle and bone, nearly breaking her foot. *Did these guys have their junk removed?* As for her simultaneous attack to their eyes, the men wore goggles of a type she'd never seen before. They were perfect protection and resisted even her hardest punches or attempts to pull them off. Two massive hulks loomed over her and then pulled out a prod of some kind—another implement she could not identify but soon felt.

She had been tasered before, but this was different. She had even been full-out electrocuted, by drug lords in Bolivia, but this was not that either. The feeling was like nothing she had ever felt, and she felt it for less time than it took for them to touch her with the weapons. She barely had time to formulate a final thought before everything vanished into the oblivion of unconsciousness. *Who are these guys?*

"I was putting groceries in my trunk," Mae replied.

"And all you saw was that damn van, goggles, and black jumpsuits—until they 'bit' you?" Tully was almost scolding.

She knew the "bit" part referred to the shock treatment. "Pretty much."

"That's all any of us saw. We all got bit hard. All of us got stuck, nabbed, and bagged. End of stories." He dismissively walked away. Mae wanted to knock his teeth out.

"Maybe we're all dead?" Sanjay volunteered out of the blue. Everyone just stared at him blankly. "I mean, maybe this is some weird limbo kind of thing and we all actually died when they took us . . . and . . ."

Ling walked over to him and punched him in the face.

Sanjay backed up, holding his jaw from the pain, "What the hell—"

"Does that feel like you're dead?" Ling asked.

Sanjay shook his head. "No."

Ling walked back to her original place. "Then shut up."

Mae made a mental note that Ling was fearless, with more than a bit of the bully in her, "What do you know?" Mae's question was not directed to anyone, but the meaning was clear enough.

"All I know is the guards don't talk, they carry these damn cattle-prod things and zap us whenever they come in," Sanjay answered.

"Have they identified themselves? Have they asked you any questions?"

"No questions. No interrogations. No contact other than the guards and that monitor." Tully surveyed the room for her, actually being helpful. "The clock sits at zero. Hasn't changed. The ceiling cameras are all lit . . ." he pointed to the little red lights on each camera, ". . . so safe to assume they see and hear all. Whoever they are. And one door in and out. That's about the size of things."

Mae had already surmised as much, but Tully was making a clumsy attempt at an "I'm sorry," and she needed to acknowledge it, "Thanks."

Ling made a pointed and clearly personal observation. "And no bathroom. I've already peed myself."

Mae looked at Tully, concerned. As military, she knew he'd understand. "No buckets, nothing?" Tully shook his head no.

"Will you two stop looking at each other in code or whatever the hell you're doing? What does that mean?" Ruby pleaded.

Mae looked rapidly around the room, "Multiple cameras with audio . . . six of us . . . only five chairs . . . so someone is always left standing . . . discomfort builds resentment . . . no latrine or buckets . . . so either we're not going to be here long enough to need them or we're going to really wish we had them in the worst way. But I don't think we're meant to be here very long."

"Why do you say that?" Michael asked.

"They let us keep our clothes," Mae answered.

Tully looked down at his own clothes. "Damn—you're right."

"So what? Maybe it means they'll just let us go," said Sanjay.

"When people take hostages," Tully replied, "or prisoners, they usually put them into jumpsuits or uniforms of some kind. It's part of the breaking resistance process. But they didn't do that with us." "So that means," Mae looked directly at a camera, as it blinked silently back at her, "we're someone's special little project."

The video monitor on the wall lit up with strange test patterns and intermittent snow.

"Shit. Here we go again." Tully stepped back as if preparing to run.

Mae watched the monitor. "What's happening?"

A voice spoke through the monitor, it was gender neutral, emotionless, commanding. Mae detected something in the voice— human but not human.

"WALLS!" The command was given. Everyone, except Mae, instantly obeyed. Clearly, they had been through this before. Each picked a wall and then stood facing it, arms to their sides, even Tully. Mae stood her ground in the middle of the room.

Tully looked at her through the corner of his eye. "Friendly advice, Mae, you might want to grab a wall." It was the first time he'd used her name. Small consolation at the moment. The camera in the ceiling focused on her. Mae's image appeared on the screen.

"WALLS!"

Mae stood still. "Fuck you," she said to herself.

Ruby stirred at her wall but didn't turn around. "Please, go to the wall! Before they come. They'll hurt us—"

The others nervously watched the door without turning their heads. Panic was setting in, but the fear of what would happen if they left the wall was obviously worse than the panic itself. *People will endure intolerable pain to avoid the uncertainty of the unknown.* Mae looked at the door. "Ruby, I think you shouldn't be talking right now."

Ruby turned from the wall to look at Mae, terrified. The monitor flickered and Ruby's picture appeared. Ruby looked up and saw her image, and the blood rushed from her face, "Oh no!"

Almost before she could finish speaking, the door slid open and two guards rushed in with long prods in one hand and a meat hook in the other.

Mae was fully prepared for battle; if this were to be the day she died, that was fine with her, but she would absolutely take these two freaks with her. But, to her surprise they only pushed her aside, knocking her to the floor, and then made a beeline for Ruby.

One guard reached out his prod and touched Ruby, which threw her hard against the wall in convulsions. Her eyes rolled up in her head, boiling in their sockets and then bursting with a violent hiss, the way cold water spits and sizzles after hitting a hot surface.

Her Raggedy-Ann body fell to the floor. The other guard pierced her shoulder with the hook and dragged her out, leaving a red streak that bisected the room from the wall to door.

The door slid closed, and the voice came back, along with Mae's picture, "THAT WAS THE FIRST —TELL US WHY."

The others stepped away from the walls and walked to the center of the room. No one spoke; they just looked at the long, red stain on the floor.

"TELL US WHY."

Tully angrily turned to Mae. "I think they're talking to you." "Why what?" Mae screamed at the monitor. "You're the one who just killed an innocent woman. You tell me 'why'!"

"IN THIRTEEN MINUTES, NUMBER TWO. YOU WILL CHOOSE. IF YOU DON'T ALL DIE."

Then silence. Mae's image switched to static, and the monitor went to black.

The old digital clock on the wall flashed and then the numbers showed: "00:13:00." The countdown began.

"What the hell is that thing doing? Thirteen minutes until what?" Sanjay asked.

Mae was thrown back in time. The circumstances had been different, the enemy then had a face she recognized, and it was a different war, but this scenario was the same as the one she had experienced in Kandahar. How that was possible, she did not know. All she knew for sure was that the past was repeating itself and —just like then—she had to survive. Mae mumbled to herself without knowing she was speaking out loud, "There is always a way out."

Michael brought her out of her thoughts, shouting, "Not for poor Ruby there wasn't!"

"Why are they asking you questions? They never asked us questions." Sanjay confronted Mae.

"They killed Ruby like a piece of meat." Ling was near tears.

"Before, they just stabbed us with those sticks. Nobody died," Michael said.

"Yeah. Not until she got here." Tully watched Mae with suspicion.

"What's that supposed to mean?" Mae asked. She knew exactly what it meant.

"I don't know. But you have something they want. None of us has ever been on that damn screen. Not until you and Ruby. And she's dead . . . and you're not. I'd kind of like to know why." Tully's challenge was unmistakable.

Mae looked up at the monitor and then off into space. "I have to think."

"Okay, good, because we've got all kinds of free time!" Tully yelled.

"What happens when it hits zero?" Ling asked, pointing to the red-on-black numbers counting down.

"Another Ruby?" Michael answered.

"Or another Michael?" Tully taunted.

"My god, you're a dick. We're in this together, you stinking, fucking, EU-loving limey." Tully went for Michael, but Mae got between them and pushed Tully back.

"This is what they want," she screamed, "and you're giving it to them. They want us to unravel." She got control of herself. "It's what they always want."

"Sounds like you've done this before," Tully said.

Mae realized she had just shown a bit of her hand and tried to cover up. "Training scenarios. I'm sure you had the same training."

"Not like this. But, then again I've heard that you Yanks like to scare the shite out of your trainees," Tully said sarcastically.

Mae could see that he was becoming more and more suspicious of her. She even began to worry that he might recognize her. After all, her picture had been in international media for at least a few news cycles. And there were Brits on her last mission—Brits she knew, broke bread with, slept with—sacrificed.

"You have to tell them. You have to tell them!" Michael pleaded.

"Tell them what? I don't know what they want!" Mae began pacing, wracking her brain trying to figure out how this was going to play out; why this situation. *Why this scenario? Why now? Why her?*

Tully grabbed her by both shoulders and pointed

her to the red numbers counting down on the wall. She wanted to collapse his larynx with a well-placed punch to the base of his neck, but she didn't. "Then in thirteen minutes," he warned, "one of us is fucked. And you get to pick which one, or we're all dead."

"So I don't think you want to be on my bad side right now—I'm just sayin'," she warned back.

Tully smiled and let her go, backing away. He had made his point. The next move was hers.

Mae stood under a camera and stared right into it as she talked defiantly. "Whatever they have planned it's going to happen in . . ." she glanced to the countdown, then back to the camera, ". . . eleven minutes and forty-two seconds."

The control room was old-fashioned, built in the 1970s, before computers and other high-tech gadgetry.

Almost all the equipment was in some level of disrepair or just plain broken. A large bank of battered video monitors lined the front wall, just above a control console filled with push buttons, sliders, gauged dials, and switches. This place was an entire order of magnitude apart from the clean, elegant, digital world the General had thrived in—before. Now, the days of clean and elegant were gone.

The General sat at the control console and watched Mae in one of the monitors. She took a long defiant pause as she stared straight into his eyes, then walked out of the frame. *Her defiance is promising*, he thought to himself. She had come to his attention just after the last war. Not the war he had just lost, but the one before that, in the days when wars were still winnable, when a military mattered. When he mattered.

He had seen her during her Congressional hearings, the kind of hearings you only get to watch if you have a need-to-know status, whose transcript pages end up almost totally blacked out from redaction, and the public's right to know is a laughable joke. He'd watched her then: defiant, calculating, word-fucking with the best lawyers on Capitol Hill and beating them at their own game. She was a clever one, this young captain, whose career was over at thirty-two, and who would be lucky to find a job in a fast food restaurant after Congress had had their way with her.

At the time, his job was to observe, assess, and report back to the other generals about her performance, her loyalty, her sense of duty. There had been some concern that after the "incident" in Kandahar, Mae might forget herself. There was trepidation that she would tell the truth of events and refuse to spin-doctor as they had coached her to do prior to her appearance before the committee. Human beings can be pushed just so far, and they break. Kandahar pushed Mae—the question was, how far? There was concern.

He had picked her for Afghanistan, and at the time all indicators showed Mae was an up-n-comer, fast-track hotshot destined for a brilliant career. He chuckled to himself, remembering what he had said to her when she accepted the mission, "Don't screw this up," and her reply, "Fuck you, General." At the moment, her reply had felt like good-ol'-boy banter, respectful insubordination, the kind of bad dialogue you hear in gung-ho action movies with candy-ass superstars playing gritty but lovable heroes.

But all the indicators were wrong. Kandahar slapped her down and chewed her up, and even knowing the truth of her survival, the General vowed never to listen to his instincts again. And after the hearings, he reported back to his superiors. She had done her duty, Captain Mae had spun a fine web for the lawyers, and she soldiered on, leaving answers nicely ambiguous and the truth lost in the fog of war. He also vowed to never see her again.

But here they were, as much by her design as his. In the darkest of days, Mae was once his greatest liability, his greatest failure. But the dark is a relative term in the face of total blackness. Now she was his only salvation.

The General caught a glimpse of himself in a dead monitor and was startled. Unshaven, disheveled, his hair a rat's nest; he barely recognized himself. And he had forgotten he was not alone. In the same monitor, he saw the shadowy figure looming to his left, sitting silent and unmoving. It was unnerving, the stillness.

The General opened a file with Mae's picture on it and laid it out on the console desk. It was filled with pictures of her in uniform, in civilian life, in combat, along with official-looking forms and paperwork.

Even sitting, the shadowy figure was not clearly visible due to its preference for low light. It lifted one of its hands and reached into the dull, yellow glow of a small console lamp that illuminated a patch of desktop in front of the General. Its hand was unnaturally long and grey, and with one cracked and hook-like finger-nail, it touched one of Mae's pictures. Its voice was the same as the voice over the monitor in the holding room.

"She tests us," it said in a breathy whisper.

The General winced at the smell of its breath, fetid and rank. "She tests everyone. I expected this. She's right on schedule. It's all in her profile." He tapped the file confidently.

"We are unconvinced," came another whisper.

"Give her a chance. She's only just arrived. She'll come through. You'll see."

The shadowy figure reached over to a button and pressed it with a bony finger, "Yes . . . let us see . . . now."

The General watched the monitor with a worried look.

◦~

The timer on the holding room clock continued its countdown, now at less than two minutes.

Mae looked at the clock and then to the others. They were all speechless, and panic filled their eyes—all except Tully, who watched Mae with interest.

"What the fuck do we do now?" Ling asked.

"Beg for our lives?" Tully deadpanned.

Mae joined them in the center of the room and shot Tully a dirty look, "When you come to a fork in the road . . . take it."

"We're gonna die and you quote Yogi Berra?" Michael nervously chuckled. "Begging, we haven't actually tried that."

Mae looked at the door intently, "That's our fork. Time to choose."

"Storm the door? Are you nuts? They'll just kill us," said Sanjay.

Mae gave Sanjay a look that left no room for doubt. "They're going to do that anyway."

"You don't know that. Wouldn't they have killed us already if they were going to?" Ling protested.

"Who are you again?" Mae responded condescendingly.

"The Chinese bitch who's going to kick your ass! You're not the only one with some experience. My husband disappeared in a combat zone a year ago . . . probably abducted and killed. So don't fuck with me, lady." Mae could see Ling was itching for an excuse to tear into her.

As much as the prospect was appealing, there was no time for that kind of thing. Tully broke the tension. "So, we jump whatever comes through that door and then make a break."

"Yes. At least some of us should make it out of here," said Mae.

"Yeah, but how far? We don't even know what's on the other side of that door," Michael's fear could be a problem, Mae thought. Everyone had to pull their weight if they were going to survive.

"Does it matter? I'm in. How do we do it? All at once?" Ling might be a bitch, but at least she had guts.

"No." Tully pulled them all up short, just as they were getting stoked to commit suicide.

"What do you mean, no?" Mae shot back.

Tully paced back and forth, thinking out loud. "They need you alive. You have something they want. So you jump the door alone and distract them. They're less likely to kill you than any of us."

They all fell silent as they considered this, as they watched the clock countdown. Mae hated to admit it, but Tully was right.

"Don't they know we're going to do this?" Sanjay almost whispered. "The cameras have mics!"

Mae looked directly at him. "Doesn't matter. All we can do is get ready."

They moved apart and Mae positioned herself strategically off to the side of the door. The ceiling cameras whirred and cranked as they recorded all the action on the floor. Their little red lights burned like hot cinders.

The digital clock on the wall hit 00:00:00.

Instantly the door slid open and a single guard entered. Mae leapt on top of him, wrestling him out of the way of the opening. In the tussle, the guard lost his dark goggles and turned to face her. Orange blood dripped from his nose holes. Mae stared into two huge, round, fish-like eyes each with a goat's rectangular pupil. Her hesitation at the sight of those eyes was enough to give the guard time to zap her with his prod. Mae's muscles seized, and her body flew off, hitting the floor like a stone, and then slid helplessly into a wall. The others were as startled as Mae was by the image of the guard standing before them. They backed up in fear as three more guards rushed into the room with their prods outstretched to quickly put an end to the pathetic revolt. Within moments the floor was littered with unmoving bodies.

Mae lay against the wall, her eyes half open and her mind half awake, unable to move. She watched as the guard without goggles picked them up off the floor and put them back on. He lifted his meat hook and walked over to an unconscious Sanjay. The guard hooked into Sanjay's thigh and dragged him from the room, leaving another red streak along the floor. As the last of the guards exited the room, Mae slipped into a numb darkness.

The monitor on the control console showed the scene in the holding room, red stains and all. The General sat back, shaken. There was a specific outcome he needed from this scenario. The variables had been factored in, the calculus made, but the damn civilian element was always a spoiler for well-made plans. It never failed: the best field actions, the tightest operations, and the most detailed maneuvers always went catty wonk when some civilian blundered into a doorway, crossed a street, or otherwise found themselves in the wrong place at the worst time. He'd lost a lot of good men and women because of the civilian factor, and it was proving to be a concern in this case. The General could not permit that. He would shoot every one of them himself, if he had to, in order to reach his outcome. There was only one life that mattered—hers.

The shadowy figure leaned closer toward the monitor, exposing some of its skin to the light, "She knew we were watching. She knew we'd stop her. Why did she do that? To what purpose?"

The General could not help but smile. He knew why. "It's what you said before: she's testing. Testing defenses, testing those people, testing our reactions. She's formulating a plan."

The figure sat back in the comfort of shadow. Its dissatisfaction was obvious.

The General grabbed a file folder and impatiently

slapped it down on the desktop under a lamp. He opened it and began reading. "Subject predictably works the odds of lost causes. In debriefs, she has consistently said that she knows she can find the win for herself in any no-win scenario. Her repeated self-talk is always, 'There's always a way out.' Libya, Yemen, Iraq, Syria, Pakistan, Kandahar—her success rate is ninety-seven per cent."

He pushed the folder forcefully closer so that the figure could see. Not that it could read anything, but his aggression might displace some of its lagging trust; they liked aggressive. But. the General didn't know how much more "explaining" he could do before even it saw through his bravado. "She's just proving her reliability. This is all consistent with what I've told you. We are completely within agreed parameters."

Two gray, gnarled hands picked up the folder and leafed through the pages. The shadowy figure leaned forward and brought its face completely out of the shadows. Its head was twice as big as a human's. The eyes were round as dinner plates and nearly as large. Unlike the guards, who were long and lanky, this one had bulk and mass. What appeared to be a large, thick jawbone curved down under scaly holes on either side of the head. There was no nose, no teeth, and no hair. As the mouth opened it resembled more the mouth-parts of a baleen whale than those of a land mammal or reptile. How it was able to speak at all was a mystery. But, speak it could.

"We move to phase two then. Know that we grow impatient. You know as well as we what is at stake," it whispered.

"All right then," the General conceded, "phase two."

The figure shifted and lifted its bulk to stand, then left the room in a limping shuffle of gray flesh and bone.

Alone, the General caught another glimpse of himself in the dead monitor glass: drained, exhausted, and nearly shattered. He looked at the monitor of the holding room and at all the bodies strewn on the floor like dolls.

Yes, he thought, *I know very well what is at stake.*

Everyone still lay unconscious on the floor, as Mae stirred and sat up, looking around. She checked the others and shook them awake one by one. Tully was the last to come back. "We're still alive," he stated the obvious.

"For now," Mae replied.

Michael glanced up at the wall clock and pointed, "Hey look." It read "oo:13:oo."

It had counted down. Mae remembered seeing the oo:oo:oo just before all hell broke loose. But now it was back to the original time—thirteen minutes. She realized what this meant, but couldn't remember. "I didn't pick anyone. Why is it back at thirteen? I didn't pick!"

She looked around quickly, counting heads. So did the others.

Then they saw the second streak of red leading to the door. "Where is Sanjay?" Ling asked, but it wasn't a question.

Tully nodded toward the second streak on the floor. "I think we're looking at him. Looks like *they* picked for you."

Michael looked at Mae's shirt and the orange stain on it. "What was that thing? Orange fucking blood?"

Mae looked down and saw the orange smudge across her clothes.

"Where the hell are we?" Michael voiced what was going through all of their minds.

Suddenly the monitor turned on and they saw Sanjay shackled to a chair, his leg was bleeding badly where the hook had punctured him. There was no sound from the monitor, but they could see Sanjay yelling from his side of the camera. His arms were tied behind him on a metal chair and his face was a pale mask of panic.

As Sanjay became more and more agitated, the entire group clustered around the monitor and watched, trying to understand what he was saying. He appeared to be glancing at something out of frame, something that clearly had him terrified. One of the guards held a piece of paper at eye level so Sanjay could read it, but he was resisting, shaking his head no.

Ling pushed her way closer to the monitor, bumping Mae out of the way, no doubt intentionally. "They're making him read something, and he's giving them a hard time," Mae yelled out loud. "Yes, Sanjay— fuck them!"

Mae spoke with authority, with the voice of someone who understood, perhaps with a confidence that even she barely accepted. "Terrorists do this all the time with prisoners. You've seen it on the news a million times. They force statements, confessions, denouncements of whatever country the prisoner belongs to. They'll probably make us do the same thing. I recommend just doing it and not giving them an excuse to kill you, or worse. You can always take back whatever bat-shit crazy thing they make you say after the fact."

Tully pushed the point. "So, you think we can get out of this alive? I thought you didn't see any percentages."

Mae paused a long time, "There are always percentages. You just have to know when they're in your favor."

Ling stepped next to Mae. as they both watched Sanjay squirm, "Did *they* ever make you say something bat-shit crazy? Did you ever just 'go along' and take it back afterwards?"

Mae looked at Ling with a cold, hard, gaze, more of

an assault than a look. For a moment, Ling's bravado appeared shaken. Mae spoke slowly, "No. I was never forced to recite anything."

As soon as she said it, Mae realized she'd exposed herself. Ling was too smart not to read between her lines; none of them was stupid. Tully's head cocked, like a dog hearing a high-pitched sound, and Michael just looked confused. But Ling pressed in. "But, someone forced you to do something. Right?"

It's hard to be impenetrable 24/7. Mae had tried it with the U.S. Congress and won. She'd maintained it with her superior officers after Kandahar when they threatened her with a dishonorable discharge and even prison. And later, she'd managed to be totally alone in the world, carrying out the mundane day-to-day on the outside and on the inside roiling and churning like lava building to a cataclysmic release.

But maybe this was the time? Maybe these were the people? Could the universe have picked a more bizarre time and place for Mae to suddenly face herself and reveal to the world her truth—*the truth*? Her mind and emotions whirled like a squall inside her, and her emotional wall lowered a bit more. *Maybe*, she thought, *maybe with these people?*

Michael broke the moment and brought their attention back. "Hey, something is happening."

All eyes went to the monitor. Another guard had come into Sanjay's room, and "he" was holding some-thing—something moving.

Tully, squinted and strained to see. "What the fuck is that? An animal?"

It was about the size of a basketball, only more oblong, wider than long. Light gleamed off its skin the way a thin film of oil reflects light off black tarmac. "Skin" was probably the wrong word, carapace was more accurate. Centipede-like legs rhythmically undulated beneath it as a guard held it off the ground by the edges of its exoskeleton, moving it closer and closer to Sanjay's chest. Something moved on the beast where a mouth ought to be, but not a mouth, more like a chitinous ribbon of clear spikes and blades. Mae had seen something similar in pictures of giant snails and mollusks, but this was neither of those. Large pincers snapped frenziedly, groping forward into space, and muscled tentacles flailed in search of something to strangle.

Mae nodded her head slightly, "I know exactly what that is."

"What?" Tully asked.

"An incentive."

The monitor's sound came on, and they could hear Sanjay's voice mixed with sharp, snapping sounds as the squirming creature was brought closer to his chest, while he read aloud the paper in front of him.

"Keener . . . Joseph . . . Sergeant First Class . . . U.S. Second Armored Division . . ." Snap, snap, snap. "Thomas . . . Henry . . . Corporal . . . U.S. 1st Infantry

Division . . ." snap, snap, hiss, "Caldwell . . . Ernest . . . U.S. Infantry Division . . ."

As Sanjay read more names, Mae instinctively turned away from the group so that they could not see her face. If they had been able to see her expression, they would have seen the shock of recognition that registered as a body blow with each name. She knew them, every one of them, and they were screaming, *Remember me!*

And then Sanjay's shrieking panic let loose the final blow, "Avery . . . Jean . . . Squadron Leader . . . Royal Air Force . . ."

Tully instantly reacted. "Avery . . . did he say, Avery?"

Michael nodded, looking numb, confused. "Yes, and Caldwell. He said, Caldwell. I have a cousin named Caldwell. He disappeared in the war, MIA. What is going on?"

He turned to Tully whose own confusion was clearing, replaced by rage, "My uncle was a Squadron Leader in the Royal. His name was Avery. He was also MIA in the war."

Ling and Michael stood silent as Sanjay began repeating the list over the monitor, even more rapidly than before. The closer the beast came to his body, the faster he read.

Tully walked over to Mae, whose back was still to the group. "Turn around."

Mae straightened and then slowly turned. She said nothing, but her face could not hide the truth.

Ling's fists tightened and her jaw clenched into a knot. "You know what's going on. Tell us—bitch."

Mae gave Ling a "bring it on" look but then softened. It was Mae's time, and they deserved to question her. They had a right to answers. Months of hiding behind lawyers, generals, and spin doctors had finally caught up with her. There was no going back to her old life, there was no going forward. There was only the moment. And even that was unravelling. But there was a part of her that was willing to let them have their fear and anger, and ultimately the rage that she knew would bury her like the fresh earth of a newly cut grave.

"Sanjay's being forced to read those names for you, isn't he? This is for you," Tully demanded.

"It's for you too." Just as she replied, Mae realized there was no longer any sound coming from the monitor. She looked up, and the others followed her gaze. The volume had been turned off, but Sanjay was no longer reading. He was screaming soundlessly, as if in some twisted silent movie. The creature was on Sanjay's torso pulling large swaths of flesh from his bleeding chest. Mae could see Sanjay forming the words "help me" as he died, piece by piece. Suddenly, the screen cut to static, to black, and then Mae's image appeared on the screen. The voice returned.

"TELL US WHY!"

Shaken, Mae moved past Tully and Michael, and then pushed past an intractable Ling and stood directly under the monitor, "I didn't pick him."

"TELL US WHY?"

"You set up the rules—I had to pick the next one. I didn't pick him!"

"YES . . . YOU DID," The voice countered.

The monitor switched images. It began a playback of the time when the group was positioned just before they decided to fight. They had recorded everything.

Sanjay asked, "Don't they know we're going to do this? The cameras have mics!"

Mae looked directly at Sanjay. "Doesn't matter. This was all planned. All we can do is get ready."

The group moved apart and positioned themselves for the attack just as the door opened and the guards entered. The playback ended. There was the hiss of static again, then Mae's image.

Mae realized the voice was right: she had picked Sanjay, not directly, but by focusing her last conversation on him she effectively "chose" him, or at least that's how she weighed the consequences in her own mind. "You tell me why," she railed at the monitor. "What do you really want from me?"

She quickly looked up at the digital clock to see if it had started counting down. There was no change—yet. The monitor went black.

Tully began to circle her the way he had earlier.

Mae really hated that. "Well, looks like they are refiguring things. Or . . ."

"Or what?" Mae asked.

"Or they're giving you more time to stew over what just happened." Tully replied.

"What did just happen?" Michael asked.

Ling joined Tully, circling Mae, but in the opposite direction. "What happened, Michael, is that poor Sanjay got eaten alive right in front of us, Ruby was butchered, and apparently we're all locked in this hell hole because of her."

Tully stopped circling, "Sounds about right."

Ling stood next to him creating a united front, "All those people are somehow connected to you . . . and we're all connected to them . . . and so whatever we're doing here right now is probably due to something you did with all of them."

"You were all together, weren't you?" Tully asked.

Mae nodded.

"From the moment you got here, I felt like you knew something—more. Something we didn't know. Like you'd seen all this before. That's because you have. We're all playing out some sick replay of the past, aren't we? Your past." Tully finally made the logical connection.

Ling exploded in anger. "Enough with the fucking twenty questions." Ling rushed Mae, grabbed her by the shoulders, and drove her bodily into a far wall. The two women slammed to the floor as Tully and Michael ran to pull Ling off of Mae. "Tell me what happened, bitch! Where is he? Tell me what you did—or I swear—"

Tully and Michael pulled Ling off, and Mae rose from the floor.

Ling pulled away from Tully and walked across the room to an opposite wall, like a boxer taking their corner after the bell. "What do you mean, where is he? Where is who?" Tully demanded.

Ling was silent, using both hands to wipe the tears from her eyes and cheeks.

Mae answered for her. "Her husband. She meant, where is her husband."

"I thought you said he disappeared," Michael asked Ling.

"He did, but as Sanjay was reading off all those names I realized you all had connections to those people. But my husband wasn't on the list. So why was I here?" She looked over to Mae. "But, he had to be there, right, with all the others—wherever you were? Otherwise I wouldn't be here."

Mae took a deep breath. "Yes."

Ling shook with emotion. "What happened? Why aren't you dead?"

The General watched the monitor and could not have asked for better timing in the unfolding of events. The shadowy figure watched him with keen interest, and the General knew that what happened next would bring the full weight of the past, present, and future down on the shoulders of one woman. He reached over, pushed a switch, and whispered to himself, "Stay strong. Stay you."

Beside him the General heard the hushed and subdued sounds of a snigger of cruelty escape thin, bloodless lips.

The monitor on the holding room wall started playing another video. Mae watched with horror as she recognized everything.

She saw a large room, a cafeteria in an old, bombed-out school. Mae never knew exactly where she had been held, but she knew it had been in Kandahar, and she knew what was coming. Her previous captors obviously recorded the whole incident in Afghanistan for later use, maybe for blackmail purposes or just because they were freaks and liked torture porn. Regardless, somehow whoever was orchestrating the present nightmare had found this piece of her past, and now it was playing for all to see, especially Ling.

On the monitor Mae watched herself standing at one end of the room and a man standing at the other end.

She held a pistol in her hand, and he was unarmed.

Mae knew the dialogue before it was even spoke it on screen.

"Go ahead. Do it," the man said, resolved.

Ling walked closer to the monitor, "That's my husband, Frank." She turned to Mae. "What the fuck did you do?"

Mae looked at her with no emotion on her face. "Watch."

Ling gave Mae a look that said *I'm going to kill you*, and then turned to the monitor.

"Come on! You fucking killed everyone else . . . just do it!" Frank goaded her.

"*They* killed them. Not me. I had no choice," Video Mae yelled back, raising the pistol.

"You picked. You followed their orders and one-by-one decided who lived or died. How did that feel, you traitorous cunt? So now it's my turn. What are you waiting for?"

Video Mae lowered the pistol. "One of us has to go back. Tell what happened."

"Then shoot yourself and be done. I'll put some nice flowers on your grave in Arlington." Frank laughed.

Video Mae raised the pistol again. Frank stiffened. "There's always a way out."

"I know." Video Mae pulled the trigger and shot Frank in the head. There was a long pause and silence on the monitor as Frank bled out onto the floor. Video Mae lifted the barrel of the pistol to her mouth but couldn't bring herself to pull the trigger. She dropped the gun just as Afghan soldiers rushed in to subdue her. The monitor went to gray static and then to black.

No sooner did Mae lower her wet eyes from the monitor than Ling was on her with both hands tightly wrapped around her neck. Mae did not resist.

Her eyes met Ling's as they collapsed to the floor. Mae saw nothing but murderous rage in Ling's eyes. She wondered what Ling saw in hers, if anything. Her old drill instructor had taught her how to break a choke hold and how to reverse the situation and kill the attacker in two quick moves. Mae could only chuckle to herself at what a disappointment she would be to him now, willingly allowing an amateur to choke her out of this world. As if in a dream, Mae watched as Tully and Michael, once again, struggled to pull Ling off her. They succeeded just as blood vessels started to burst in Mae's eyes

and stars of hypoxia sparkled around her.

As the world returned to her, Mae gagged and coughed up blood. She heard shrieks of expletives and curses spewing from Ling's mouth, every other word being "bitch." Tully and Michael had to virtually sit on Ling to keep her restrained.

Mae looked up at one of the ceiling cameras with hate in her eyes. Its little red light burned as if to laugh at her pathetic attempt at redemption. Whoever was looking back at her knew exactly how to play her. They had from the start.

"TELL US WHY!" The voice cut through the chaos of the room and everyone froze for a moment before standing up and facing the monitor.

Mae finally lost it, grabbed a plastic chair, and hurled it at the monitor. "You don't want to know why . . . you motherfuckers. You could care less—why! What you want is a confession!"

She turned to Ling, Michael, and Tully. "That's what you all want, too. *All right, I confess!* You want to know why I'm alive and they're all dead? Because I'm a fucking survivor. That's what I've always done. I live. I survive—fathers who can't keep their dicks in their pants, husbands who can't keep their fists to themselves, commanders who want me dead just because they don't want a woman in combat, and terrorists who want me dead . . . just because."

Her outburst took whatever energy she had left, and she dropped to her knees in exhaustion. "I get out alive . . . that's what I do . . . that's what I am."

Tully walked over to her, looking as drained as Mae. They were all completely spent.

"Because there is always a way out," he said.

"Yeah. There is always a way out. For me."

Suddenly the monitor comes alive again. "SHOW US."

The monitor went dead. Tully turned to Mae with terror on his face. "Fuck."

May looked at him, truly not understanding.

"You just gave them what they wanted," Tully said.

"So, what—" Mae realized the *what* as soon as the word left her mouth. She looked to Michael and Ling with regret in her eyes. "Now they don't need us," Michael said matter-of-factly.

No sooner did he say that than two guards rushed into the room with sticks and meat hooks.

They first took Michael, hooking him through the neck, dragging him gurgling and spitting blood from the room. Then Tully was hooked through the chest, without the benefit of being stunned, and dragged out of the room. He made eye contact with Mae the whole time and was still alive when he disappeared into the deep darkness of the corridor. But the door did not close behind him.

Ling and Mae were the last ones standing. They looked at one another, unsure what to do. Mae made a move for the door, but two more guards rushed in and stood on either side of it. Now they were holding weapons akin to rifles, but different. The monitor came alive once again.

"KILL THE OTHER. ALL WILL LIVE. OTHERWISE, ALL DIE."

Ling started to laugh. "Isn't this poetic—or some fucking cosmic joke? You get to kill me and my husband the same way. He was right, you are a traitorous cunt."

Mae looked at Ling calmly. "I'm not killing anyone." She raised her hands showing they were empty.

One of the guards reached inside a deep pocket in his jumpsuit and pulled out a pistol and slid it to her along the floor.

"SHOW US . . . OR ALL DIE."

Ling stepped back in fear. Mae picked up the gun, looked at Ling and then at the monitor, "'All' . . . there's only the two of us left, you sick fuck." She pointed the gun at the guards and emptied the clip into both of them. The guards took the bullets and bled orange blood, but they remained standing.

Mae threw the gun at one of them, and he caught it midair with one elongated hand. He then reached into another pocket, pulled out another pistol, and slid it back to Mae.

Ling chuckled. "Well . . . looks like they've got your back. My husband was a hero . . . the bravest man I knew. And loyal. Something you couldn't possibly know. Because as long as you have a gun in your hand, you have a way out. Right? But . . ."

"But what?" Mae asked the question, but there was a disingenuous quality to it. Deep down, in places where Mae knew the truth lurked waiting like a siren calling her toward the rocks in an angry and punishing sea, she knew Ling was on to her.

"There's a better way."

Mae was at the end of her resistance. "Maybe I don't want out this time."

"It's what you do. What you are, remember? So, finish what you started—" Ling said.

"I . . ." Mae could not finish her statement. There was no clever comeback, no snarky bite or verbal parry. Her pause hung heavy in the air between them.

"On the monitor. You put the gun to your mouth but didn't pull the trigger." Ling paused, then came to the point. "Finish what you started."

Tears ran down Mae's face, but no one would ever have thought she was crying by looking at her face. It was a mask, unfeeling, lifeless. But the tears—

Ling was opening a door for her, one she had fantasized about for months, but could never walk through.

Mae looked at the guards, then at the ceiling camera, then at Ling. "I'm a survivor. As long as I have a gun in my hand, there's a way out. You said it yourself. And, you're right. I'm sorry, Ling. I'm so very sorry. For everything. For all of it."

Ling steeled herself. But then Mae tossed the gun to Ling, who caught it and immediately pointed it at Mae. The guards made no move to stop them.

"What are you doing? Is this some trick?" Ling asked.

"Finishing what I started, Ling. You can do it. I couldn't then, I can't now. But, you can. You're the only one who can. You're the only one who should." Mae smiled. "It's your way out. Take it. And forgive me."

Ling smiled back, but it was not a nice smile. "No, I don't think I will." She paused—a bit too long.

A bright flash filled the room, followed by a loud

buzzing sound, and Mae found herself suddenly covered in white ash. She barely had time to wipe the ash from her eyes when she was grabbed by the guards and pulled kicking and screaming from the room.

As the door slammed behind her, Ling softly rained down out of the surrounding air like fine confetti.

She would have recognized an interrogation room if it had been inside a big cardboard box. They all looked the same: barren, unforgiving, suspicious, persecuting. In this case, the room was small, probably an office converted for the purposes of "intel gathering." That's what Mae and her colleagues had called it when they "interviewed" prisoners. Only now she was the intel.

Mae scanned the room for the hundredth time, no windows, a flimsy aluminum table and two old-style metal chairs. There were no handcuffs on her, but there was a large American soldier outside the door with an AK-47 and a pissy attitude. Even if she were able to kill him, where would she go? Whoever was smart enough to pull off this horror show was smart enough to find her and do the whole dance all over again. No, Mae wanted to see this through to the end; she owed it to the others. All the others, and there had been so many. They had cleaned her up, afterwards, but ash is hard to get rid of. It finds its way into every crevice, between all the hairs, up nostrils, and under fingernails. Ling would be with her for a very long time.

Mae was trained to compartmentalize emotions. That had always been one of her strengths. Being able to turn off and turn on one's capacity to feel and care for others was a talent shared by sociopaths and professional soldiers. *Okay, maybe that's the same thing*, she thought. But. this time, during this "situation," that talent had failed her. Mae was still unsure why, or how, but it had. The thing that shocked her most was not that emotion ruled her. It was rather the other way around: what was shocking was that it was okay with her. She liked it. It was proof—she was still human.

Her DI would have kicked her ass from pillar to post for admitting such a thing, but it was the truth. Mae did not know why all this had happened or why the military was involved—and it *was* the military; otherwise the crew-cut outside the door would have one of those monsters with orange blood, not a government-issued, tow-head blond. But she knew something now that she hadn't known when she was dumped into that damn room: she could still feel regret. Her thoughts were interrupted by the sudden realization that the door was open and that someone was watching her silently from the doorway.

The General stood for a moment and nodded to the guard, who closed the door behind him. He carried two files and put them neatly on the table.

Mae noticed that his hair was uncombed and he had several days of beard growth. His uniform was wrinkled and messily arranged, and it looked like there were bloodstains on the lapels of his jacket. He wore no fruit salad on his chest, which is unusual for official military, but he did have the single silver star insignia of a brigadier general on both tips of his shirt collar. She searched her memory but could not remember him.

"You don't stand and salute your superior officers anymore, Captain?" the General asked.

Mae hesitated and sat there looking up at him. "Fuck you, General."

He laughed and sat down across from her. "That's exactly what you said to me the first time we met. Nice to see some things never change."

"We've met before?" Mae could not place his face.

He answered evasively as though he had something to hide, and changed the subject, "Yes. I imagine the guards who cleaned you up filled you in a bit on what's been happening?"

"They were pretty talkative, considering they're not supposed to say anything to prisoners. I am a prisoner, right?"

He looked down at one of the folders and opened it. "Yeah, well, military discipline isn't what it used to be. As for being a prisoner . . . Mae, may I call you Mae, we're way past that, I'm afraid."

"So monsters with orange blood have taken over

the planet. Funny, I didn't see anything about that on the news."

"No, you wouldn't have. We kept it pretty quiet. But you saw some of that blood for yourself, didn't you?" He pushed the folder toward her.

Mae thumbed through the pictures slowly. "I've seen a lot of blood today, General."

"Yes . . . you have."

Mae hardly knew what to make of the images in front of her. These weren't the Hollywood-alien-invasion pictures everyone was accustomed to, with massive spaceships hovering over big cities, or ray guns blasting monuments apart, or fleets of alien invaders blacking out the sun with overwhelming armies of robot drones. These were images of conference rooms at the White House, the situation room, the U.N., the Kremlin, and Beijing. Business meetings with generals, politicians, and tall, gray forms looming over puny humans who seemed cowed and beaten. If this was an invasion, it was a stealth job, done behind closed doors, with meeting agendas, minutes taken, and action items on to-do lists. This was an attack of bureaucrats, not warriors.

"I don't understand," Mae said flatly.

"Six months ago, they made contact. On a cell phone, if you can believe that." The General reached over and moved some pictures aside to show satellite images and military surveillance of fleets of spacecraft in near-Earth orbit. "I can't pronounce their name.

Their language is . . . well. . . anyway . . . they contacted the militaries of all the big powers. As you can see, they demonstrated their superiority, told us to submit or die. It was all over in thirteen minutes. That's how long it took to conquer the human race—thirteen minutes."

"Thirteen minutes—what? Was that a joke with the clock?" She was angry.

"Thirteen minutes is a day on their world. They thought it would be funny, a little inside joke. It seems they have a sense of humor." The General sneered.

"This is insane. What am I doing here? Why were we all here? Why did all those people have to die?"

He closed the file and slid the other one over to her —the file that mattered, the one that made sense of all the madness. "What's this?" she asked.

"The why." The General sat back as Mae slowly looked through the file. Unredacted and uncensored, her life unfolded before her in old polaroid pictures, photocopies of psych evals, select printouts of emails to ex-husbands and boyfriends, even an old handwritten shopping list. The "why," she kept repeating in her mind.

"They do this a lot, apparently. Go to a world, conquer the native population, steal all the natural recourses, but they don't necessarily kill everyone first. They see if there is some compatibility. Some shared values. Makes for better slaves, I guess. So the defeated are given a choice: demonstrate worthiness . . . or be . . . vaporized."

She looked at him disbelieving. He almost chuckled. "Yeah, I know, turns out aliens do have death rays after all."

"Demonstrate worthiness how?" Mae asked.

"I can't speak for other civilizations, but in our case, our demonstration was—you."

Like responding to the combination to a lock, the tumblers fell into place. Her subconscious must have been chewing on his comment that they had met before. Now she remembered. "Afghanistan. You son of a bitch."

The General was almost apologetic in his tone. "I know . . . I was one of the people who picked you for Kandahar. I was there at your inquiry when you got back. Never forgot your case. Turned out your performance was perfect."

"A performance? Is that what it was to you?" Mae asked.

"More of an audition, really." He smiled slightly as he said it.

She didn't know whether to reach across the table and snap his neck or just beat the crap out of him. One of the two was imminent.

He seemed to sense her mindset, almost welcoming it. "You can take the girl out of the battlefield, but you can't take the battlefield out of the girl, eh?"

But then a strange weariness covered him like a thick blanket, and he looked past her as though she weren't there. As he spoke, she felt that he was speaking to someone else, making a case, reassuring a stranger.

"Everything said you'd save yourself. Every psychiatrist, all psychological indicators, *everything* pointed to you being a predictable subject." He touched her file and finally made eye contact. "It's all in here. All the data. All your selfishness, self-centeredness, self-importance, the 'me-first' attitude. It's all here. Always a way out. Alpha dog, survivor. You ask me why? *You were the why.*"

Like a junkie beginning to fall into a withdrawal, the General started trembling, and tiny beads of sweat formed on his brow and upper lip, "These creatures . . . they're very much show-me-the-money people. We told them—hey, we can get along, we think like you do, we're advanced, we have computers and space travel after a fashion—but they came back with 'show us.' And then they told us what we needed to demonstrate. They gave very precise parameters, qualities, traits, behaviors. As soon as I heard their requirements, I remembered you, my sure bet."

"You're not answering my question—demonstrate for what purpose?"

"You—and the others. I needed predictable, I needed repeatable, I needed the familiar. What better way to show what we needed to tell them than banking on a sure bet?" He pointed to the profile folder again. "It's all there. Just like Afghanistan, you or them. I needed you to be you." The weariness was replaced by a deep sadness, almost a regret that was unspoken. Mae wasn't sure, but it looked as though tears were forming in his eyes.

Mae shoved the folder back toward the General and scattered the paperwork all over the floor. He made no move to pick it up. "Well," Mae chided, "here I am. You got what you wanted. I hope the price was high enough for you. You got something out of me that all the torturers and the U.S. Congress never could. I confessed. I killed those men. Just like I killed those people in there. You got what you wanted. Now let me leave."

The General sat back and looked at her for a while, saying nothing. Finally, he stood and moved toward the door. "Take a walk with me."

Mae hesitated but saw he was serious, so she joined him and followed him into the hallway. The guard was gone, and there was no evidence of another human being anywhere nearby. They walked down the hall to a set of double doors and the General opened them to a clear-skied night, black as velvet, with stars twinkling overhead. He led her out onto a small balcony that overlooked a small park of trees, grass, and walking paths. The lights of a town could be seen in the near distance, though there were no sounds of cars or people. *Curious*, Mae thought. But it was wonderful to feel the night air again on her face and breathe fresh air.

As they both looked out over the city lights, the

General became somber, "So, you learned from your mistake."

"What?"

"Afghanistan. Killing Ling's husband to save yourself. It changed you."

Mae had never stated it quite so clearly in her own head, but that was what had happened, "Yes. I suspected as much, even before your little science experiment. But I didn't really know it until Ling told me to finish what I started. Then I knew. I deserved to die."

The General nodded his head. "Remorse. Truly feeling sorry."

"I'd never felt either of those—before. And you denied me the rest. I was ready. Why didn't you let her do it?"

The General laughed. "I didn't stop it. They did. They wanted to see if you would make the same choice."

"Well, this time I made the right choice. I made the human choice." Mae's voice was confident, resolved.

The General straightened his messy tie and buttoned his jacket, trying to make himself more presentable, "Yes. You made the human choice. But that was the wrong choice."

"What the hell are you talking about?"

"They don't respect compassion," he said, "or love, or being sorry. They hate weakness. They see humans as soft and worthless. They like selfish. They respect winners. I told them you were the model human. We were all like you, deep down inside. They wanted to see . . . they demanded to see. So I gave them you. Our last chance. Our best bet."

"So I failed their test. Then why not just let Ling kill me? Why drag this out? Why take that away from me?" Mae knew she sounded as though she was begging, but she no longer cared.

"Remember, I said they had a sense of humor? Well, they thought it would be funny to let you see the endgame. Just how big our gamble failed. Real jokers, those guys."

Mae finally understood. "'All die' . . . they didn't mean all of us in the room . . . they meant . . ."

"Humanity." The General nearly choked on the word. He looked off into the distance. The town's lights were going out. A loud, mechanical buzzing filled the air. Flashes of bright light went off in the blackness. The General finished making himself look like a professional once again. He combed his hair back with his fingers and rubbed the stubble on his cheeks with his hand. "I needed you to be you. The you in those files. We all needed you to be that person. But you changed. You found your humanity."

The flashes of light grew closer, the buzzing louder.

Mae was crying. She stared off into space at the brightening light show and mumbled, "But, I made the human choice."

The General pulled a small handgun from his inside jacket pocket. "Yeah, I really wish you hadn't done that."

He turned and walked back into the building, leaving Mae alone to watch the ending of the world. From inside the hallway, Mae heard a single shot from inside the hallway. As the lights grew closer and brighter, they slowly washed out Mae's field of vision, but not before she felt the gentle flutter of white ash on her cheeks, like the first dusting of an early snow.

THE END

ABOUT THE AUTHOR

Jeff Lyons is a published author and story consultant with more than 25 years of experience in the publishing and entertainment industries. He has worked with literally thousands of screenwriters and novelists, including *New York Times* and *USA Today* bestselling authors. His writings on the craft of story-telling can be found in leading trade magazines like *Writer's Digest Magazine, Script Magazine,* and *The Writer Magazine,* among others. His book, *Anatomy of a Premise Line: How to Master Premise and Story Development for Writing Success* was published by Focal Press in 2015. Jeff is a popular presenter at leading writing industry trade conferences, and has been invited to present and consult for the annual Producers Guild of America's "Power of Diversity Producers Fellowship Program," as well as for the Film Independent Screenwriting Lab. Jeff lives in Long Beach, California, has one weird cat, and desperately wants a dog. Visit www.jefflyonsbooks.com.

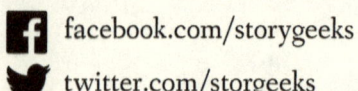

facebook.com/storygeeks

twitter.com/storgeeks

instagram.com/jefflyonsbooks

AUTHOR OFFER—ANATOMY OF A
PREMISE LINE

AVAILABLE ON ALL MAJOR ONLINE
BOOKSELLERS

*"Every writer on the planet needs coffee,
chocolate, and this book!"*

— CAROLINE LEAVITT: NEW YORK
TIMES BESTSELLING AUTHOR OF
IS THIS TOMORROW

[SEE NEXT PAGE]

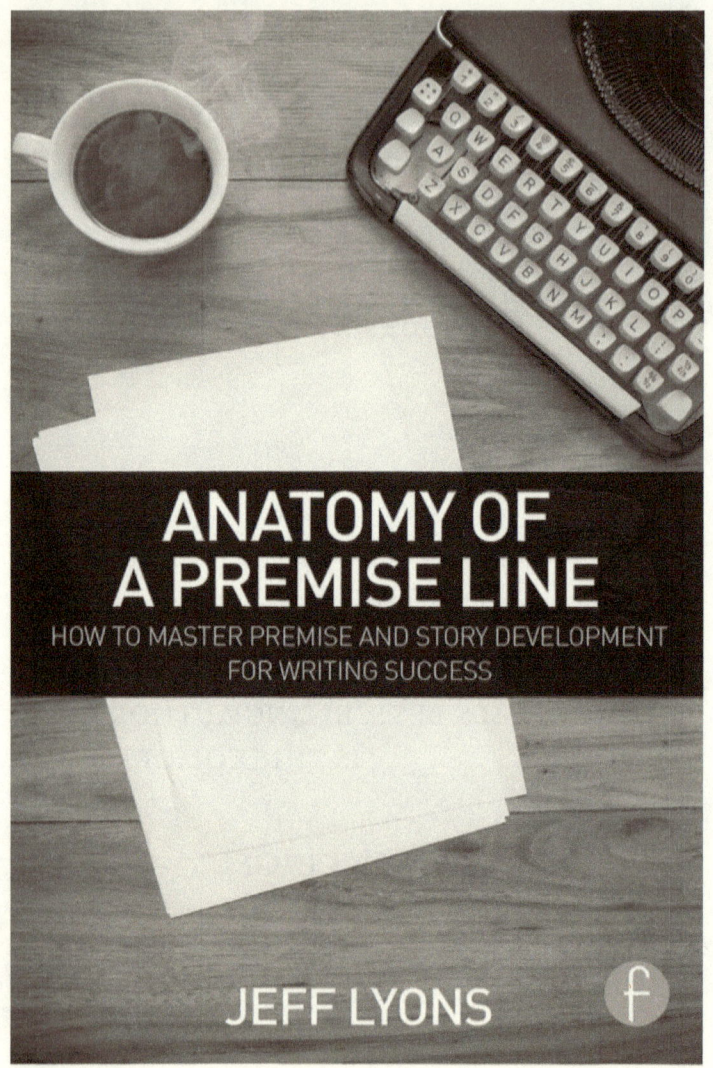